The Hermit and the Well

Plum Blossom Books ✦ P.O. Box 7355 ✦ Berkeley, CA 94707 ✦ www.parallax.org

Plum Blossom Books is an imprint of Parallax Press, the publishing division of Unified Buddhist Church, Inc.
© 2003, by Unified Buddhist Church, Inc. ✦ All rights reserved. ✦ Printed in China.

Illustrations by Vo-Dinh Mai. ✦ Jacket and text design by Gopa & Ted 2, Inc.

ISBN 1-888375-31-0

Library of Congress Cataloging-in-Publication Data

Nhât Hanh, Thich.
  The hermit and the well / by Thich Nhat Hanh ; illustrated by Vo-Dinh Mai.
      p. cm.
  Summary: While on a school field trip in Vietnam, a young boy climbs a mountain without finding the
Buddhist hermit he is expecting to see, but later realizes that he has found much more.
      ISBN 1-888375-31-0 (pbk.)
  [1. Buddhism—Fiction. 2. Hermits—Fiction. 3. School field trips—Fiction. 4. Vietnam—Fiction.] I. Vo, Dinh
Mai, ill. II. Title.

PZ7.N4887He 2003
[E]—dc22   2003015176

1 2 3 4 5 / 07 06 05 04 03

THE Hermit
AND THE Well

Thich Nhat Hanh

ILLUSTRATED BY VO-DINH MAI

PLUM BLOSSOM BOOKS ✦ BERKELEY, CA

When I was a child, I lived in North Vietnam.
One day, our school teacher told the class that we
were going on a trip to the top of a nearby mountain.

He said that at the top of the mountain there lived a hermit — a man who lived alone and sat quietly day and night to become peaceful like the Buddha. I had never seen a hermit before. I was very excited.

The day before the trip, we made
food for a picnic. We cooked rice,
rolled it into balls, and wrapped
the balls in banana leaves.
We prepared sesame seeds, peanuts,
and salt to dip the rice in.

The morning of our trip, we walked for a long time
until we reached the foot of the mountain.
My friends and I climbed as quickly as we could—
we ran almost all the way up the mountain.

There were many beautiful trees and rocks along the path. But I did not stop to look at them because I wanted to reach the top of the mountain. I ran past flowers and trees. I rushed past the bright blue sky.

When my friends
and I finally reached
the top, we were very tired.
We had drunk all of
our water on the way
and did not have
a single drop left.

We looked around for the hermit.
We looked and looked. Then we saw
his hut made of bamboo and straw.

Inside, we discovered a small cot
and an altar made of bamboo, but no hermit.

Where was he?

Maybe he had heard us
coming up the mountain
and was hiding somewhere
away from the noise. It was time
to have lunch, but I wasn't hungry.
I was too tired and disappointed.

Maybe if I wandered into the forest I could find
the hermit. I left my friends and started climbing
further up the mountain. I was very thirsty.

As I walked deeper into the forest,
I heard the sound of dripping water.
It was like the sound of music being softly played.

I started to climb in the
direction of that lovely sound.

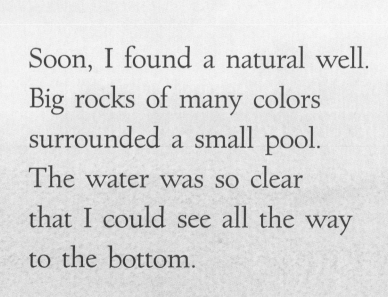

Soon, I found a natural well.
Big rocks of many colors
surrounded a small pool.
The water was so clear
that I could see all the way
to the bottom.

I knelt down, scooped some water in my palms, and began to drink. The water tasted wonderfully sweet. You cannot imagine my happiness. It was delicious!

I felt completely satisfied.
I did not need or want
anything at all—
even the desire to meet
the hermit was gone.

But suddenly I realized I may have met the hermit after all.
Maybe the hermit had transformed himself into the well.
Maybe he cared about me. This made me happy.

I lay down on the
ground next to the well
and looked up at the sky.
I saw the branch of a tree
against the blue sky.
I was very relaxed.

Soon I fell into a deep sleep.

I don't know how long I slept. When I awoke, I didn't know where I was.

Then I saw the branch of the tree against the sky and the wonderful well. I remembered everything.

It was growing dark and
it was time to go back to
join my classmates.
I said good-bye to the well
and began to
walk back down.

As I walked out of the forest,
a sentence formed in my
heart. It was like a poem with
only one line:

"I have tasted the best water

in the world."

My friends were glad to see me. They asked me
where I had been, but I had no desire to talk.
I wanted to keep my story to myself for a moment.
I sat down on the ground and ate my lunch quietly.

The rice and the sesame seeds tasted so good.
I felt calm, happy and peaceful.

That was many years ago
that I climbed that mountain.
Now I am an old man.
But the image of the well
and the sound of dripping
water are still alive inside me.
You too may have met your hermit.
Maybe it was a rock,
a tree, a star, or a
beautiful sunset.

The hermit is the Buddha
inside of you.

Plum Blossom Books

Plum Blossom Books publishes books for young people on mindfulness and Buddhism by Thich Nhat Hanh and other authors. For a complete list of titles for children, or a free copy of our catalog, please write us or visit our Website:

Plum Blossom Books
Parallax Press
P.O. Box 7355
Berkeley, CA 94707
www.parallax.org
Tel: (800) 863-5290

Practice Opportunities with Children

Families and children are especially welcome at the Plum Village Summer Opening, where monastics and lay people practice the art of mindful living. For information, please visit www.plumvillage.org or contact:

Plum Village
13 Martineau
33580 Dieulivol, France
info@plumvillage.org

Green Mountain Dharma Center
P.O. Box 182
Hartland Four Corners, VT 05049
Mfmaster@vermontel.net
Tel: (802) 436-1103

Deer Park Monastery
2499 Melru Lane
Escondido, CA 92026
Deerpark@plumvillage.org
Tel: (760) 291-1003